# The Not So Special Bug

## Hannah Fulks
Illustrated by: Marianne Abenoja

The Not So Special Bug
Copyright © 2023 by Hannah Fulks

All rights reserved. No part of this publication may be reproduced, distributed, or transmitted in any form or by any means, including photocopying, recording, or other electronic or mechanical methods, without the prior written permission of the author, except in the case of brief quotations embodied in critical reviews and certain other non-commercial uses permitted by copyright law.

Tellwell Talent
www.tellwell.ca

ISBN
978-0-2288-8891-8 (Hardcover)
978-0-2288-8890-1 (Paperback)

To Charlie and Colbie
You light up my life.
Love, Mama

There once was a little bug.
He slept all day and was
awake all night.

The little bug thought he was not so special. What was so great about being awake while the rest of the world was asleep? He wished he could be a more special bug.

"I wish I was a honeybee", said the bug. "Bees make delicious, golden honey all day long. Bees are so special."

"Perhaps I could be a beautiful butterfly", thought the bug. "Butterflies look so fascinating flying around in the sunshine. They are so special."

"Maybe I could even be a grasshopper. Grasshoppers can jump for miles and miles on their strong legs. They are so special", said the little bug. The little bug decided he was definitely not so special.

One evening as the bug was flying around in the moonlight he noticed something shiny. It looked like hundreds of shining stars had fallen down to the earth. He flew as quickly as he could toward the sparkling lights and when he got closer, he was amazed! They weren't stars at all. They were bugs!

Hundreds of bugs were flying around with their bottoms glowing and twinkling like tiny lanterns. These were surely the most special bugs he had ever seen!

One of the glowing bugs flew over to him and said "Hello there little friend! Where have you been?" "What do you mean?", asked the little bug. "You belong here with us of course!", said the glowing bug. "I don't think so" said the little bug, "I'm just a not so special bug."

The glowing bug just laughed and laughed. "Sure you are! You are a firefly just like us! See there." he said as he pointed to the little bug's bottom..

To the little bug's surprise, he was glowing and twinkling just like the other fireflies. He flew around as fast as he could shouting with joy and shining his light. The little bug could hardly believe he was a firefly. He had been a very special bug all along.

After all, there aren't any not so special bugs.

The end

Printed in the USA
CPSIA information can be obtained
at www.ICGtesting.com
LVHW071149171023
761168LV00032B/716